Better Move On, Frog!

Ron Maris

Julia MacRae Books
A DIVISION OF WALKER BOOKS

© Ron Maris 1982
All rights reserved
First published in Great Britain 1982
by Julia MacRae Books
A division of Walker Books Ltd
87 Vauxhall Walk
London SE11 5HJ

British Library Cataloguing in Publication Data
Maris, Ron
Better move on, frog!
I. Title
823'.914 [J]   PZ7
UK ISBN 0-86203-083-8

Reprinted 1983, 1984, 1985, 1989, 1990

Printed and bound in Italy by L.E.G.O., Vicenza

For Pat Hutchins

Holes! Lots of holes!
Which one shall I have?

Better move on, Frog.
This hole is full of badgers.

Better move on, Frog.
This hole is full of rabbits.

Better move on, Frog.
This hole is full of owls.

Better move on, Frog.
This hole is full of mice.

Better move on, Frog.
This hole is full of bees.

But look!

Better move in, Frog.
And wait for the hole to fill up...

…like all the other holes.